SKOKIE PUBLIC LIBRARY
W9-DJP-551

YOUR PAL FRED

Michael Rex

VIKING

VIKING
An imprint of Penguin Random House LLC, New York

First published in the United States of America by Viking,
an imprint of Penguin Random House LLC, 2022

Visit us online at penguinrandomhouse.com.

Library of Congress Cataloging-in-Publication Data is available.

Manufactured in China

ISBN 9780593206324 (hardcover)
ISBN 9780593206331 (paperback)

1 3 5 7 9 10 8 6 4 2

TOPL

Design by Kate Renner
Text set in Out of Line BB

The artwork in this book was created in Photoshop.

To my father, who was, above all, kind.

HOT L

WELCOME To The FUTURE!
THE FUTURE STINKS

CHAPTER 1

CHUGGA!
CHUGGA!
CHUGGA

STAY DOWN UNTIL IT PASSES!

CHUGGA! CHUGGA! CHUGGA!
LET'S GO!

HERE! THIS LOOKS GOOD!

GO ON, GET IN!
CREEK!

THOSE RUST BRAINS WON'T FIND US IN HERE.

CRUNK!

LET'S HIDE
DOWN THERE.

I WONDER WHAT
THAT SIGN SAYS.
TOYS

I COULD BE WRONG,
BUT I HOPE IT SAYS
IT'S TIME TO EAT!

I'M HUNGRY,
TOO!
!

MY LUMP-LOAF
IS GONE!

IT MUST HAVE
FALLEN OUT
WHEN WE
WERE RUNNING!

NOT MY
PROBLEM.

GIMME YOURS!
I'M HUNGRY!
NO WAY!
YOU LOST
YOURS!

GIMME IT!

POW!
BANG!
BOP!
DONK!
BAM!

I GOT IT!
IT'S ALL MINE!

NOT FOR LONG!

WHIIIIP!
WHOA!

Whooooo!

CRASH!
BOOM!
THUNK!
BEEP! BEEP!

BEEP! BEEP!

BEEP! BEEP!

BEEP!
YOUR PAL FRED
BEEP!

BEEP!
BEEP!

BEEP!

BEEP!

BEEP!

BEEP!

HELLO!
THANK YOU FOR ACTIVATING ME. MY NAME IS FRED, AND I WANT TO BE YOUR PAL!
HA!
HA!
HA! HA!

WHAT'S A *PAL?*
A PAL?

A PAL IS SOMEONE YOU ENJOY BEING AROUND.

A PAL IS SOMEONE YOU LIKE, AND WHO LIKES YOU!

A PAL IS SOMEONE YOU SHARE GOOD TIMES WITH, AND WHO HELPS WHEN THINGS GET BAD.

OH! YOU MEAN, LIKE, A *FRIEND?*

EXACTLY! A PAL IS A FRIEND. YOU'RE VERY SMART!

I'M HERE TO BE YOUR FRIEND, AND HELP YOU LEARN HOW TO MAKE NEW FRIENDS.

HA! HA! HA!

MINE!

POW!

WHY ARE YOU TWO FIGHTING?
BAM!
BOP!

WE FOUND TWO LUMP-LOAFS, BUT I LOST MINE.
WELL, I DIDN'T LOSE MINE, SO I GET THE LOAF!

IT LOOKS BIG ENOUGH FOR TWO. WHY DON'T YOU SHARE?

HA! HA! HA! HA!

BAM!

I'M NOT SHARING WITH HIM, EVEN IF HE *IS* MY BROTHER!

YOU TWO ARE BROTHERS?

YEAH. I'M PLUG.
AND I'M PUG.

EVEN IF WE DID SHARE, HE'D BE A GREEDY GOOBER AND TAKE A BIGGER PIECE!

WHAT IF I SHOWED YOU A WAY YOU COULD SHARE THAT WAS TOTALLY EVEN?

IT'S NOT A TRICK?
YOU BETTER NOT STEAL OUR LOAF, PAL!

I WOULD NEVER DO THAT! STEALING IS WRONG!

UM . . . OK.

SO, YOU'RE GOING TO SHOW US A WAY TO SHARE . . .

. . . AND WE BOTH GET THE SAME AMOUNT?

YUP! LET'S ALL TAKE A DEEP BREATH AND HAVE A SEAT.

CHAPTER 2

NO WAY! HE'S GONNA CUT A BIG PIECE AND A TINY PIECE!

AND, PLUG, YOU GET TO CHOOSE THE FIRST PIECE.

SO I CUT THE LOAF . . .
. . . AND I GET TO CHOOSE THE FIRST PIECE.

YES!

SO IF HE CUTS A BIG PIECE AND A LITTLE PIECE . . . I CAN TAKE THE BIG PIECE?

RIGHT!
BUT I DON'T WANT HIM TO GET A BIGGER PIECE THAN ME. SO I'LL . . . I'LL CUT THEM . . . THE SAME SIZE!

AND WE BOTH GET THE SAME AMOUNT!

YOU GOT IT!

YOU'RE A GENIUS!

NOM! NOM! NOM!

DO YOU WANT ANY?

NO, THANK YOU! THAT WAS VERY KIND OF YOU TO ASK, BUT I DON'T EAT FOOD. I DON'T PEE OR POO EITHER. I'M LOW-MAINTENANCE!
HA! HA!
HA! HA!

FOR LEARNING HOW TO SHARE, I'M GOING TO GIVE YOU EACH A STICKER.
WHAT'S A STICKER?
F

BZZZZZ!

YOU'RE A STAR!

?

WAY 2 GO!

?

WOW.
YOURS IS A LITTLE STAR.

YOURS LOOKS LIKE A HAND WITH THE THUMB STICKING UP.
YUP! THUMBS-UP!
CRASH!
F

VREEE
THEY FOUND US!!

CHAPTER 3

VWOOOOP!
FRED!

ZOOOP!
AAAAHHHH!!
YIKES!
EEEEE!
VOOSH!

POOT!
URGH!
OOF!
BAM!
WHAT JUST HAPPENED?
WE GOT BAGGED, FRED!

ARE WE IN JAIL? DID WE DO SOMETHING WRONG?
NO, WE DIDN'T DO ANYTHING WRONG.
EXCEPT CHOOSING A LOUSY PLACE TO HIDE.
STOP

YOU ARE NOW ALL SUBJECTS OF THE GREAT **LORD BONKERS**, AND WILL BE SERVING IN HIS MIGHTY ARMY OF SUPERBAD DESTRUCTION!

LORD BONKERS!

WE'RE IN AN ARMY? WE'RE KIDS!

LET'S MOVE OUT! WE GOTTA CATCH SOME MORE DIRT-FOLK!

CHUGGA!
CHUGGA!
CHUGGA!

THIS IS AWFUL!
BUT THERE'S NOTHING WE CAN DO ABOUT IT!
BWOOP! BWOOP!

WHAT'S HAPPENING?
OH NO!

CHUGGA!
CHUGGA!
CHUGGA!
VROOOOM!
CHUGGA!
CHUGGA!
CHUGGA!
VROOOOM!
CHUGGA!
CHUGGA!

ARE THEY COMING TO SAVE US?
NO! THEY WANT TO STEAL US!
CHUGGA! CHUGGA! CHUGGA!
VROOOOM!

POOM!
WHIZZZZZ!
BAM!
SKREE!

YANK!
RRRIIIIPPP!!
OOF!
AAAHHH!
F

GRAB MY HAND!
PLUG!

OOOOF!
URG!
BONK! DONK!

RRRRRR

HUH?

RRRRRR

GRAB!

GRAB!

WHAT NOW?

WE'RE BAGGED AGAIN!

OOF!
URK!
VROOOOM!

MORE JAIL?
YEAH, THIS TIME WE'RE—
WELCOME ABOARD, BOZOS!

YOU ARE NOW ALL LUCKY MEMBERS OF **PAPA MAYHEM'S** ULTRA-UNSTOPPABLE CYCLONE OF CHAOS!

WHAT'S THAT?
ANOTHER ARMY.

LORD BONKERS AND PAPA MAYHEM HAVE BEEN SNATCHING UP ARMIES FOR A FULL-ON WAR WITH EACH OTHER.

AND WE'RE THE SOLDIERS?
YUP.

I DON'T WANT TO BE IN AN ARMY.
NO ONE DOES.

HEY!

RRRIP! RRRIP!

YOU STOLE MY WRENCH.

YEAH? SO WHAT? I'M A THIEF! STEALING IS WHAT I DO, AND I'M GETTING OUT OF HERE!

GIMME IT BACK! IT BELONGS TO MY BROTHER!
LOOK, DIRT-BOY! WE CAN FIGHT, OR WE CAN ESCAPE!

HEY! THERE'S NO NEED TO FIGHT! I'M SURE WE CAN WORK SOMETHING OUT!

VROOOOM!

DONK!
VRO

OOPS!
NOT AGAIN!

VROOO

OOF!
POOM!
HERE'S YOUR BROTHER'S WRENCH BACK, BUDDY!

YAA!
ZOOF!

PUG!
JUMP!
I'M
COMING!

WHOOSH!
CLANG!
I'M STUCK!

OH NO!

VROOOOOM!

I GUESS WE'RE NOT WORTH COMING BACK FOR.

CHAPTER 4

ARE YOU GOING TO THANK ME FOR SAVING YOU, KID?
UM, YES! THANK YOU.

IT WAS VERY THOUGHTFUL OF YOU. MY NAME IS FRED.

I'M WORMY, AND NOW YOU OWE ME ONE.
ONE WHAT?

YOU'VE GOTTA DO SOMETHING FOR ME SOMETIME.

YES! I SHALL RETURN THE FAVOR! IT WILL BE MY PLEASURE TO DO SOMETHING FOR YOU, WORMY.

YOU'RE VERY PROPER, AREN'T YOU?
IT'S HOW I'M PROGRAMMED.

YOU'RE
A ROBOT?
YES! I AM AN ARTIFICIAL
INTELLIGENCE PROGRAMMED
TO SPREAD KINDNESS,
FRIENDSHIP, AND GOOD VIBES!

HAW! HAW!

SO, YOU'RE NOT MADE
TO HUNT PEOPLE, OR STOMP
THINGS OR EXPLODE THINGS?

I WOULD NEVER
DO ANYTHING
LIKE THAT.
I'M HERE TO
MAKE FRIENDS.

WOW.
YOU'RE THE
DUMBEST
ROBOT EVER.

I DON'T SEE IT
THAT WAY. BUT
IF THAT'S YOUR
OPINION, I'LL
ACCEPT IT.

THEN I CAN GET MY NEW FRIENDS, PUG AND PLUG, OUT OF THOSE ROTTEN ARMIES. BROTHERS SHOULDN'T BE SEPARATED!

!?!?!

YOU'RE GOING TO ASK LORD BONKERS AND PAPA MAYHEM TO DO WHAT?
TO STOP FIGHTING.

THEY SHOULD BE FRIENDS! NONE OF THESE AWFUL THINGS WOULD HAVE HAPPENED IF THEY GOT ALONG AND WERE KINDER TO EACH OTHER.

HAW! HAW! HAW!

FRED, YOU'VE GOT BUGS IN YOUR SKULL!

THERE'S NO WAY THOSE TWO KNUCKLEHEADS WILL EVER STOP FIGHTING! THEY'VE BEEN GOING AT IT FOR YEARS!
YEARS? REALLY?

YEAH, THEY'VE BEEN BATTLING OVER LAND AND RESOURCES AND FOLLOWERS SINCE BEFORE I WAS BORN.

NOW THEY WANT TO HAVE ONE GIANT ALL-OUT WAR! THEY'LL NEVER STOP FIGHTING, FRED! IT'S WHAT THEY DO!

WELL, I BELIEVE THAT MANY PEOPLE WOULD BE HAPPIER IF THEY WEREN'T FIGHTING.

LISTEN UP, ROBOT BUDDY-BOY . . .

LOTS AND LOTS AND LOTS OF PEOPLE WOULD BE MUCH HAPPIER WITHOUT THOSE TWO MEGA-NUTS BANGING AWAY AT EACH OTHER ALL THE TIME. BUT THAT'S A DREAM, FRED. A DREAM THAT WILL NOT COME TRUE.

BUT . . . HAS ANYONE ACTUALLY ASKED THEM NOT TO FIGHT?

IF THEY DID, THEY'RE NOT ALIVE ANYMORE TO TELL THE STORY.

OH! THAT'S FRIGHTENING!

YES, FRED, FRIGHTENING! THEY'RE WARLORDS! THE WORST RULERS "THE ZONES" HAVE EVER SEEN!

FRED, THIS IS A ROUGH WORLD, AND I THINK YOU MIGHT BE TOO INNOCENT FOR IT. MAYBE YOU SHOULD JUST DIG A HOLE AND HIDE IN IT FOR AS LONG AS YOU CAN.

I COULD NEVER HIDE IN A HOLE WHEN THERE ARE SO MANY UNHAPPY PEOPLE AROUND.

WHATEVER, FRED.
ONE MORE QUESTION?

WHO LIVES CLOSER? LORD BONKERS OR PAPA MAYHEM?

LORD BONKERS.
THREE DAYS.
THAT WAY.

THANK YOU,
WORMY!

F

BE
KIND

LA LA LA . . .

CHAPTER 5

LEE LA LOO . . .
BEEP BOP BOO . . .

LA LA . . .

LOO . . .
GO BACK

WHOOOOOOOOO!

WHOOOOOOOOO!
LA LA LA . . .
LEE LEE . . .
LOO LA LEE . . .

I SAID
GO BACK
ZOOBY DOOBY WOO . . .

CHAPTER 6

LEE LEE LEE . . .

LOO LA LEE . . .

HI, I'M FRED. I'M LOOKING FOR LORD BONKERS. DOES HE LIVE AROUND HERE?

HA! HA! HA!
HA! HA! HA!

NO, FRED! THE BIG MAN DON'T LIVE HERE.

HE'S IN THAT DIRECTION, ANOTHER DAY OR SO. BUT IF I WERE YOU, I'D TURN AROUND . . .

. . . AND GO THE OTHER WAY.

FAST!
THIS AIN'T NO PLACE FOR A KID.

THANK YOU FOR YOUR CONCERN, BUT I REALLY NEED TO SEE LORD BONKERS.

HAVE A NICE DAY!

"HAVE A NICE DAY"?
"THANK YOU FOR YOUR CONCERN"?

HA! HA!
WHAT A LITTLE KOOK!

LA LA LA . . .

?

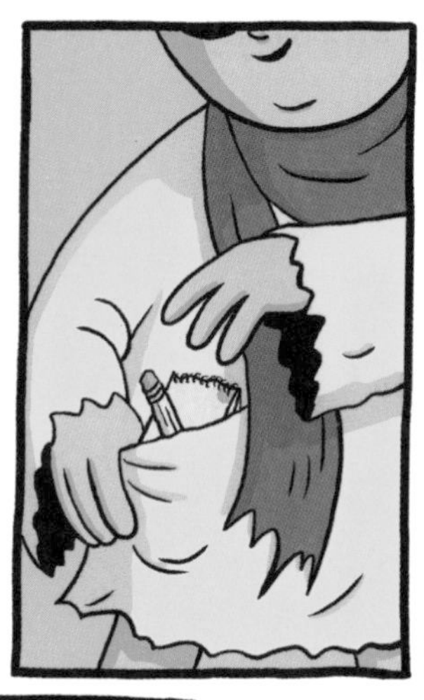

FRED!

WORMY!
HELLO!

HOLD THIS!

HOW LONG SHOULD I HOLD IT?

YOU LITTLE BRAT! GIMME BACK MY SPUDS!

HELLO!
WHOMP!
I DIDN'T EXPECT THAT!

WHOMP!
OR THAT . . .
WHOMP!
OR THAT EITHER . . .
OOOF!

YOU'VE GOT THIS COMING, YOU THIEVING LITTLE RUNT!
WOW! I REALLY LIKE YOUR HELMET! IT'S SUPER NEAT!
DON'T TRY TALKING YOUR WAY OUT OF THIS!
I'M BEING HONEST! IT'S A COOL HELMET. THE BEST I'VE SEEN!

REALLY?
YEAH! WHERE DO YOU GET A HELMET LIKE THAT?

I MADE IT!
YOU MADE IT? YOU'RE REALLY CREATIVE!

YOU THINK SO?
YEAH!

HUH . . .

I THINK YOU'RE VERY TALENTED. WAS IT HARD TO MAKE?
IT WAS! FIRST I HAD TO GATHER ALL THE PIECES AND PARTS.

THEN I HAD TO SEW THIS . . . AND CONNECT THESE . . .

THEN I CUT THIS . . . AND I PAINTED THAT . . .

WOW! YOU'RE A TRUE CRAFTSMAN! YOU SHOULD BE PROUD OF THE WORK YOU'VE DONE.

REALLY?

HEY! WAIT A SECOND! ARE YOU JUST BEING NICE TO ME SO I DON'T CRUSH YOU FOR TAKING MY SPUDS?

NO! I WOULDN'T LIE TO YOU!

I THINK YOUR HELMET IS AMAZING, AND I'M VERY IMPRESSED WITH YOUR SKILL AND IMAGINATION!
AWW! GEE, THANKS!

I THINK THESE ARE YOURS.

HEY! THEY'RE NOT HIS!

HE STOLE THEM FROM SOMEONE ELSE! I SAW IT!

REALLY? WHY WOULD SUCH A TALENTED PERSON NEED TO STEAL ANYTHING?

IT'S HARD OUT HERE IN THE DUNES. IT'S WHAT EVERYONE DOES, KID. YOU STEAL AND YOU ROB AND YOU BONK PEOPLE. I DON'T LIKE DOING IT, BUT IT'S HOW I SURVIVE.
HMMM . . . I THINK YOU'RE BETTER THAN THAT.

I THINK YOU'VE GOT TO TAKE ALL THAT CRAZY CREATIVITY YOU'VE GOT IN THIS HEAD OF YOURS . . .

. . . AND DO SOMETHING SPECIAL WITH IT!
TAP! TAP!

I THINK HE'S JUST ANOTHER DUSTY WASTELAND CROOK WHO ONLY KNOWS HOW TO STEAL AND CHEAT.
THAT'S NOT VERY NICE.

SHE'S RIGHT.
I'M A JERK.

HERE, KID, YOU
KEEP THE SPUDS.

I'M OUT
OF HERE!

SORRY I BONKED
YOU SO MANY TIMES.
I GOT A BIT RATTLED,
BUT IT DOESN'T HURT.

BZZZZ!

I'M A GOOD EGG!

THIS IS FOR YOU.

YOU'RE A GOOD EGG.

CHUGGA!
CHUGGA!
CHUGGA!

CHUGGA!
CHUGGA!
CHUGGA!
JAILTRUCKS! SEE YOU AROUND, KID!
MY NAME IS FRED!

YOU CAN CALL ME JUNKBOY!
NICE TO MEET YOU, JUNKBOY!

CHUGGA! CHUGGA! CHUGGA!
UH . . . WHERE SHOULD I GO?

HEY, FRED!

CHUGGA!
CHUGGA!
CHUGGA!

CHAPTER 7

WE NEED TO STAY OFF THE BUSY TRAILS SO WE DON'T GET BAGGED AGAIN.

YOU'RE RIGHT! WE DON'T WANT THAT!

SO, YOU'RE STILL ON YOUR WAY TO SEE LORD BONKERS?

OF COURSE! IF I CAN GET LORD BONKERS AND PAPA MAYHEM TO BE BUDDIES, MAYBE PEOPLE WON'T HAVE TO STEAL EACH OTHER'S FOOD.

FRED, THEY ARE NEVER GOING TO BE BUDDIES! IT'S NOT HAPPENING.

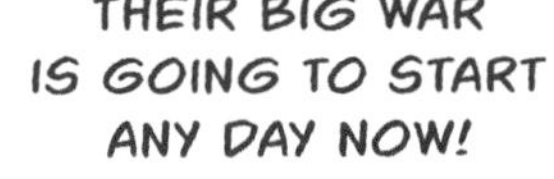
THEIR BIG WAR IS GOING TO START ANY DAY NOW!

THEN I HAVE TO
WALK FASTER!

HUP, HUP, HUP!

LA LEE LOO . . .

HELP!

HELLO? IS
SOMEONE THERE?

DO YOU
HEAR THAT?

FORGET IT.
IT'S NOTHING.

HELLLOOOO?

I AM DOWN HERE.

OH!
HELLO THERE!

CAN YOU HELP ME?

I CAN TRY.

WHY ARE YOU HELPING
THAT STUPID OLD BOT?

IT DIDN'T DO
ANYTHING
FOR YOU!

THAT DOESN'T MATTER.
IT NEEDS MY HELP, SO
I'LL SEE WHAT I CAN DO.

THAT'S NOT HOW THE WORLD
WORKS ANYMORE, FRED! YOU HAVE
TO TAKE CARE OF YOURSELF
AND ONLY YOURSELF! NO ONE
ELSE MATTERS!

I DON'T SEE THE WORLD
THAT WAY, WORMY.

SKITCH

SO, WHAT SEEMS TO BE THE PROBLEM, PAL?

I CANNOT STAND UP.

MY PULSE GYRO IS GETTING NO POWER.

I HAVE NO IDEA WHAT A PULSE GYRO IS . . .

. . . BUT I'LL DO MY BEST TO FIGURE IT OUT.

HMMMM . . .

NOM! NOM!

GOTCHA!
COME ON OUT!

YOU'RE NOT SUPPOSED TO BE IN THERE!

IT SEEMS LIKE THIS LITTLE CUTIE LIKES MUNCHING ON YOUR WIRES.

GO CHEW ON SOMETHING ELSE,
MY SLIPPERY LITTLE FRIEND.
SKRIT!
SKRIT!

I THINK I CAN FIX YOU NOW.

CLICK!
CLACK!

WHIRRRR!

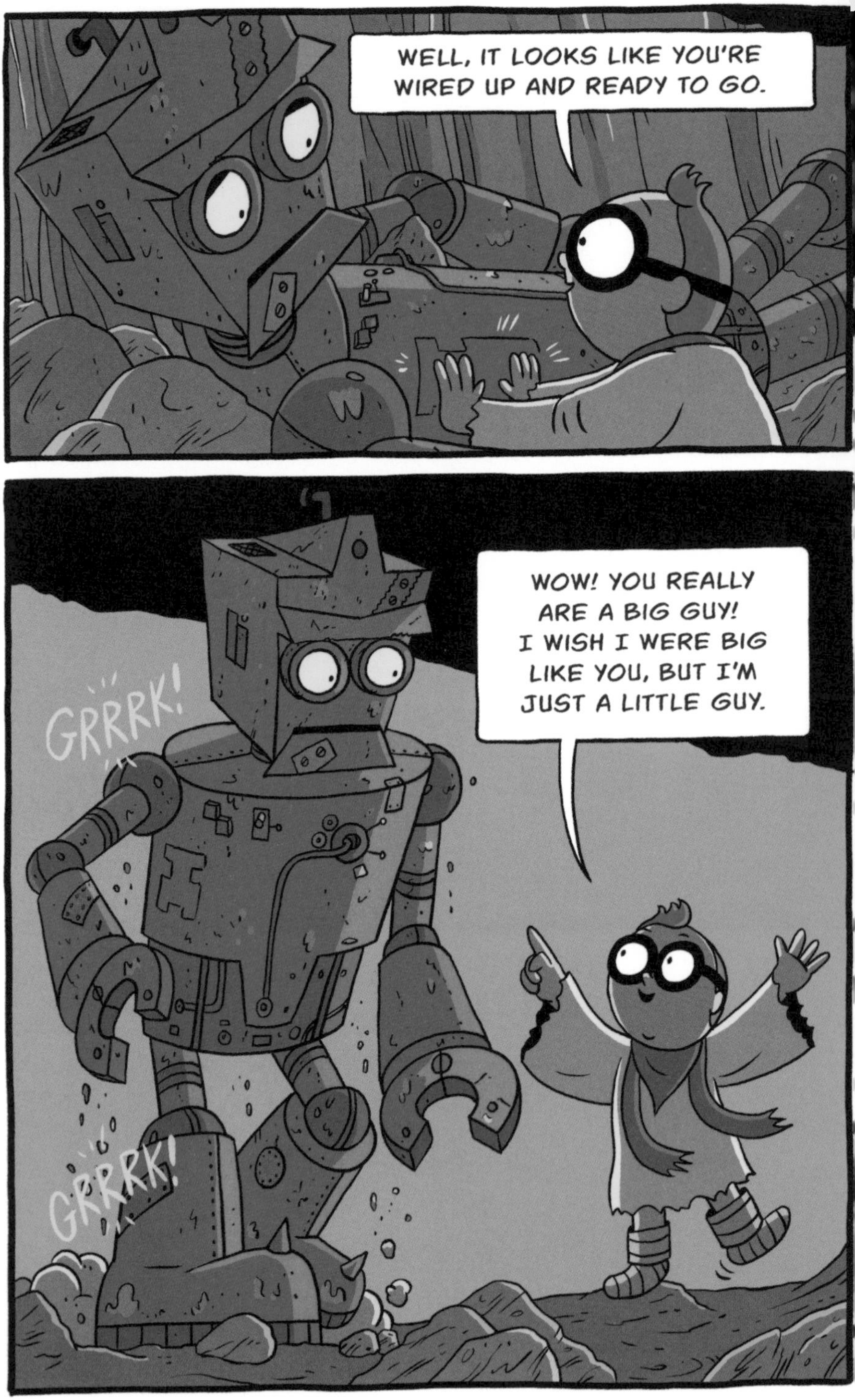

GRRRK!

WOW! YOU REALLY ARE A BIG GUY! I WISH I WERE BIG LIKE YOU, BUT I'M JUST A LITTLE GUY.

GRRRK!

THANK YOU, LITTLE GUY. YOU ARE VERY KIND. MANY WOULD HAVE TORN ME APART FOR SCRAP AND LEFT ME TO RUST.

OOH! THAT DOESN'T SOUND LIKE FUN.

I'M FRED. WHAT'S YOUR NAME?

I HAVE NO NAME, FRED.

NO NAME? WHY NOT?

I AM JUST A WORKER WITH NO NEED FOR A NAME.

HMMM . . .

WELL, I'M GOING TO CALL YOU "YUMMY."

THAT IS A STRANGE NAME, FRED. WHY WOULD YOU CALL ME YUMMY?

BECAUSE THAT LITTLE CRITTER SURE THOUGHT YOU WERE YUMMY.

SOME MAY FIND THAT AMUSING, FRED, BUT I DO NOT.

GOODBYE, FRED. I MUST GO.

I AM SURE MY MASTER IS LOOKING FOR ME.

I DO NOT WISH TO ANGER HIM.

GOODBYE, YUMMY!

STOMP! STOMP! STOMP!

MISSION ACCOMPLISHED!
GOOD FOR YOU. ARE YOU HUNGRY?

IT'S GONNA BE YUMMY!

CHAPTER 8

YOU'VE BEEN DRAWING THAT SYMBOL ALL OVER THE PLACE. WHAT IS IT?

I'VE NEVER SEEN IT BEFORE.

YOU'VE NEVER SEEN THIS BEFORE?
NOPE, NEVER.

IT'S A HEART.

YOU MEAN THE THUMPY THING IN YOUR BODY THAT MAKES BLOOD?
YUP.

THAT DOESN'T LOOK ANYTHING LIKE A HEART!

I GUESS IT REALLY DOESN'T, DOES IT?

WHY DO YOU PUT IT EVERYWHERE? DOES IT MEAN SOMETHING?

IT MEANS "LOVE" AND "KINDNESS" AND "FRIENDSHIP" AND "SHARING" AND ALL OF THE THINGS THAT MAKE US FEEL WARM . . .

. . . AND SQUISHY.

FREDDY! YOU SILLY BOY! NOW I KNOW WHY I'VE NEVER SEEN THAT STUPID SYMBOL ANYWHERE! NO ONE BELIEVES IN THAT GOOFY JUNK ANYMORE.

I BELIEVE IN THAT GOOFY JUNK.

AND SOMETIMES ALL A PERSON HAS IS WHAT THEY BELIEVE IN.

WELL, YOU BELIEVE IN WHAT YOU WANT, FRED!

I BELIEVE IN GETTING WHAT I WANT, WHEN I WANT IT, ANY WAY I CAN GET IT!

HEY!

WE'RE HERE.

WOW! NEAT!
WELCOME TO LORD BONKERS'S FORTRESS.

LET'S GO!

THIS IS GOING TO BE UGLY.

IT WOULD BE NICE IF I BROUGHT HIM A GIFT.

YOU MEAN A TRIBUTE?
NO, JUST A LITTLE GIFT. A SIMPLE TOKEN OF OUR NEW FRIENDSHIP.

LIKE WHAT?

HMMM . . .

OOH! I KNOW!

LOOK AT THIS ROCK! IT HAS A CUTE LITTLE FACE ON IT.

SEE THE LITTLE FACE?

YOU'RE GOING TO GIVE LORD BONKERS, THE RULER OF THE BROKEN VALLEY, A ROCK WITH A LITTLE FACE ON IT?

YUP! AND HE WILL LOVE IT!

IS THIS THE LINE TO SEE MR. BONKERS?

LORD BONKERS, YOU LITTLE HALF-BRAIN.

OH YES! RIGHT.

JUST GET IN LINE AND ZIP IT, KID!

I CAN DO THAT.

UM . . .

I'M OUT OF HERE, FRED.
YOU'RE NOT COMING WITH ME?

NAH . . . I'M NOT REALLY INTO MEETING A WARLORD.

THANK YOU FOR ALL OF YOUR HELP, WORMY!

LA LA LA . . .

CHAPTER 9

HELLO! MY NAME IS FRED! IT'S REALLY NICE TO MEET YOU, LORD BONKERS!
GIVE ME MY TRIBUTE! NOW!

TRIBUTE? I DON'T UNDERSTAND.

PUT THE TRIBUTE YOU BROUGHT ME ON THE FLOOR!

WELL, I DIDN'T BRING A TRIBUTE, BUT I DID BRING YOU A LITTLE GIFT.

PLOP

CLANK!
CLANK!
CLANK!

WHAT... IS... THAT?

IT'S A ROCK I FOUND.

IT HAS A LITTLE FACE ON IT, SEE?

HEY THERE, LORD BONKERS!

MY NAME IS ROCKY McCUTIE-CUTE!

I WANT TO BE YOUR NEW BEST FRIEND!

ENOUGH!

UH-OH! WHERE DID HE GO?

PEEK-A-BOO! I SEE YOU!

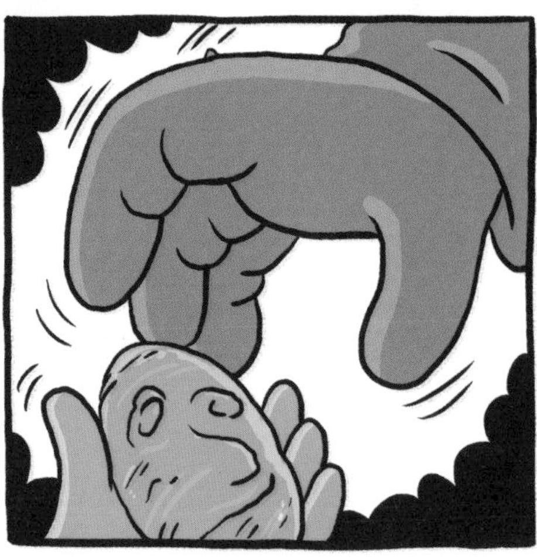

CRACK!
CRUMBLE!

WHAT KIND OF POO-BRAINED IDIOT ARE YOU?

GEE! I'M KINDA NEW TO THIS PLACE. I GUESS I JUST GOOFED.
BUT MAYBE I DO HAVE SOMETHING ELSE FOR YOU!
WHAT COULD YOU HAVE THAT I COULD POSSIBLY WANT?

HOW DARE YOU?! YOU COME INTO MY KINGDOM WITHOUT A WORTHY TRIBUTE, AND THEN THINK YOU CAN OFFER ME YOUR PITIFUL . . . **FRIENDSHIP?**

!

GUARDS! RUN HIM UP
THE ROD!

YEAH!
THE ROD!

BUT EVERYONE
NEEDS FRIENDS!

?

YANK!

ZOOOOOOOSH!
CRACK!

ZAP!
HOORAY!

WOOOOO
YOU GUYS LOOK LIKE ANTS FROM UP HERE!

HE'S NOT SUPPOSED TO ENJOY THIS!

LA LA LA . . .

CRACK!

WOOOOOOOOOO!

HELLOOOOOOO?
CRACK!

I HAVE SOMETHING FOR LORD BONKERS.

IF I BRING YOU DOWN, YOU'LL HAVE TO GO BACK UP!

THAT'S OKAY!

YOU CAN LEAVE ME UP THERE AS LONG AS YOU WANT.

THANKS!

WHAT IS THIS?

CHAPTER 10

I'M SORRY TO DISTURB YOU, BUT THAT WEIRDO ON THE ROD ASKED ME TO GIVE THIS TO YOU.

"DEAR LORD BONKERS, THANK YOU FOR TAKING THE TIME TO TALK WITH ME. I'M SURE YOU ARE A VERY BUSY GUY. IT WAS NICE TO SEE YOUR EXCELLENT THRONE ROOM. IT'S VERY BIG AND IMPRESSIVE. I WOULDN'T WANT TO MOP THAT PLACE! HA! HA! THANKS AGAIN, YOUR PAL, FRED."

WHAT IS THIS?

HE SAID IT WAS A "THANK-YOU LETTER."

WAIT, THERE'S MORE . . .
"I FORGOT TO SAY THAT I HOPE WE CAN TALK AGAIN SOMETIME SOON. I HAVE A VERY IMPORTANT QUESTION THAT I WOULD LIKE TO ASK YOU. THANKS, AGAIN, YOUR PAL, FRED."

HE'S GOT A HEAD FULL OF MUCK.
BUT HE'S SO FULL OF MUCK THAT I WANT TO HEAR WHAT HE HAS TO SAY.

WE COULD ALL USE A GOOD LAUGH.

BRING HIM DOWN!
RIGHT AWAY, LORD BONKERS!

GOOD MORNING.
LORD BONKERS WANTS TO SEE YOU!

SO, FRIENDLY FRED, WHAT IS IT THAT YOU WOULD LIKE TO ASK ME?

WELL, I WAS WONDERING IF YOU WOULD DO ME A FAVOR?

HA! HA! HA!

FRED, YOU SEEM LIKE A NICE YOUNG BOY. UNWISE, FOOLISH, MAYBE EVEN HALF-BRAINED . . . BUT NICE.

SO, I MIGHT ACTUALLY CONSIDER DOING A LITTLE, ITTY-BITTY FAVOR JUST FOR YOU.

BOOP!

OH! THANK YOU SO MUCH, LORD BONKERS.

I WAS WONDERING . . . WELL, IT SEEMS THAT EVERYONE IN THIS WHOLE VALLEY WOULD BE A LOT HAPPIER IF THEY WEREN'T BEING GRABBED UP AND HELD PRISONER AND MADE TO BE SOLDIERS, AND—

GET TO THE POINT, FRED!

OOPS.
ULP!
URK!
IF YOU'D LIKE ME TO HELP YOU BECOME FRIENDS WITH HIM, I WOULD BE GLAD TO DO THAT.
HOW DARE YOU COME INTO MY KINGDOM AND MENTION THAT HORRIBLE NAME!
THE BOOT! THE BOOT!
GIVE HIM THE BOOT!

THE BOOT!
THE BOOT?
STAND HERE, KID!
BEGONE!

WHOOOOSH
AND NEVER COME BACK! YOU WRETCHED LITTLE FOOL!
?

WHAM!
WOOSH!
THAT WASN'T THE REACTION I WAS—

DONK!
—HOPING FOR.
CONGRATULATIONS, FREDDY! YOU SURVIVED THE BOOT!
YOU KNEW ABOUT THE BOOT?
EVERYONE KNOWS ABOUT THE BOOT.
THAT'S HOW I KNEW YOU'D END UP HERE . . . GIVE OR TAKE A HUNDRED FEET.

THAT MEETING DIDN'T GO VERY WELL . . . HMMM, WHAT'S NEXT?

WHICH WAY DOES PAPA MAYHEM LIVE?
SMACK!

NOW YOU WANT TO GO SEE MAYHEM? YOU DON'T KNOW WHEN TO GIVE UP, DO YOU?

WHY WOULD I GIVE UP? I WANT EVERYONE TO BE HAPPY!

YOU DON'T LEARN, FRED! MAYHEM'S WORSE THAN BONKERS! YOU'LL NEVER GET OUT OF HIS FORTRESS ALIVE.

RRRRRRRR
RRRRRRRR
HUH?
GRAB!
GRAB!
NOT AGAIN!

AAAAHHHH!
EEEEEK!
RRRRRRRRRRRRR!
UGH!
OOF!
HELLO, SIR!

COULD YOU PLEASE TELL ME—
SIT DOWN AND ZIP IT, KID! YOU ARE NOW THE PROPERTY OF THE BIG DADDY OF THE WASTED WORLD, PAPA MAYHEM!

FANTASTIC! I'M FRED. WHAT'S YOUR NAME?
MY NAME? MY NAME IS GREASY MO!

NOW STOP BOTHERING ME, PUNK!

GOOD NEWS! WE'RE ON OUR WAY TO PAPA MAYHEM'S.
GREAT. AT LEAST WE DON'T HAVE TO WALK.

I LIKE THAT POSITIVE THINKING!

NOW WE JUST HAVE TO GET OUT OF THIS JAIL TRUCK AND TALK TO PAPA MAYHEM.

YOU CAN FIGURE THAT OUT YOURSELF. I'M GOING TO SLEEP.

DO YOU WANT ME TO SING YOU A LULLABY?
NO, FRED.

DO YOU WANT ME TO TELL YOU A BEDTIME STORY?
NO, FRED.

I WANT YOU TO STOP MOVING YOUR MOUTH SO I CAN SLEEP!

UM . . . COULD YOU TELL US A BEDTIME STORY?

YOU BET! EVERYBODY GET COMFY!

ONCE UPON A TIME . . .
RRRRRRRRRR!

RRRRRRRR!
HOTE

CHAPTER 11

PRESENTING TODAY'S CATCH FOR "THE RULER AS FAR AS THE EYE CAN SEE AND EVERYTHING BEYOND," THE BIG, BAD BROSKI HIMSELF, **PAPA MAYHEM**!
MOVE IT, YOU FILTH-GLOBS!

HOORAY FOR ME!

HELLO, PAPA MAYHEM. HOW ARE YOU?

I'M FINE, THANKS. HOW ARE—

SILENCE!

NO ONE MUST EVER SPEAK TO PAPA MAYHEM!

OOPS! MY BAD! I JUST WANTED TO SAY HELLO.

I SAID SILENCE!

YOU'RE WEIRD!

OH, SPOON OF TRUTH! THIS KOOKY LITTLE BOY INTRIGUES ME . . . DO I TALK WITH HIM . . . OR DO I TOSS HIM IN THE DUNGEON?

OK . . . YEAH?

HE'S TALKING TO A
SPOON AND HE THINKS
YOU'RE WEIRD?

GUARDS! LOCK UP ALL THESE RUNTS,
BUT LEAVE THE STRANGE ONE HERE!

DON'T WORRY
ABOUT ME.

C'MON, YOU
LUNKHEADS!

SO, WHO ARE YOU AND WHAT DO YOU WANT, CHATTY LITTLE BOY?
WELL, I'M FRED. IT'S VERY NICE TO MEET YOU, MR. MAYHEM. THANK YOU FOR TAKING THE TIME—

I ASKED YOU WHAT YOU WANTED!

ANSWER NOW! NOW, NOW, NOW, NOW, NOW!

WELL, I'D LIKE TO TALK TO YOU ABOUT AN IDEA I HAD.

OH! YOU HAD AN IDEA, DID YOU? IN THAT PERFECTLY ROUND HEAD OF YOURS?

I WAS WONDERING IF YOU AND LORD BONKERS—

LORD BONKERS?!

PTOOEY!

PTOOEY!
PTOOEY!

NEVER!

EVER!

EVER!

EVER!

EVER!

NEVER SAY THAT HORRIBLE, ROTTEN, MISERABLE, JIVE-TURKEY NAME AGAIN IN THE KINGDOM OF PAPA MAYHEM!

YOU HEARD HIM! NEVER AGAIN!

ULP!
HA! HA! HA!

WHEN YOU WALKED IN HERE, I KNEW YOU WERE DIFFERENT!
I KNEW YOU WERE STRANGE! BUT I DIDN'T KNOW YOU WERE . . . KOOKY!

BUT YOU, FRED, ARE KOOKY! YOU ARE KOOKY-BAZOOKY AND ALTOGETHER OOKY! YOU'RE THE KOOKIEST KOOK I EVER MET!
BOOP!

SO TELL ME MORE ABOUT THIS
KOOKY IDEA, FRED . . . THIS "MAKING
PEOPLE HAPPY AND NOT FIGHTING."

WELL, IT'S
SIMPLE . . .

YOU AND THE OTHER GUY,
WHO I ALREADY SPOKE
TO, WOULD JUST, YOU
KNOW . . . STOP FIGHTING.

HUH. YOU ALREADY
SPOKE TO
LORD BONKERS?

I THOUGHT WE
SHOULDN'T SAY
HIS NAME.

I CAN SAY IT.
I CAN DO WHATEVER
I WANT.

I CAN EVEN WEAR MY HAT ON MY BUTT, SEE?

LIAR! I THINK YOU WENT TO HIM FIRST BECAUSE YOU'RE A SPY!
WHAT? NO!

BYE-BYE, FRED THE SPY! YOU'RE GOING TO THE BOOM ROOM!

TO THE BOOM ROOM!
CLICK!

CLICK!

YIKES!

BYE-BYE!

CHAPTER 12

WELCOME TO YOUR NIGHTMARE!
WELCOME TO INSANITY!
BOOM! BOOM!

BOOM
-BA-
BOOM!
WELCOME TO . . .
THE BOOM ROOM!
BOOM!
BOOM!

HEH-HEH!
BOOM!
BOOM!

BOOM-BA-
BOOM!
YOU'RE A
GREAT
DRUMMER.
BOOM!

NO!
I AM NOT!
I AM YOUR
DOOM!

BOOM
BOOM!
STOP DANCING!
BOOM!

BUT IT'S A GREAT BEAT!
NO! IT IS NOT! IT IS DESIGNED TO DRIVE YOU . . .
BOOM!
BO
BOOM!

. . . KOOOOKY!
WELL, I LIKE IT!
BOOM -BA- BOOM!
BOO

HE'S DANCING! THAT LITTLE WEIRDO IS DANCING IN THE BOOM ROOM!

WHO DANCES IN THE BOOM ROOM?

WHEN PAPA MAYHEM DROPPED ME DOWN THAT NASTY CHUTE, I THOUGHT I WAS IN FOR SOMETHING BAD.

YOU ARE! MY DRUMMING DRIVES PEOPLE MAD! I DO NOT STOP! I CAN DRUM FOR DAYS. MOST PEOPLE WHO ARE SENT HERE CAN ONLY LAST A FEW HOURS. SOME HAVE TRIED TO LAST LONGER . . .

BOOM

BOOM

BOOM-

BOOM -BA- BOOM!

IT IS WHAT
I DO!

BUT DO YOU LIKE IT?
I . . . I NEVER THOUGHT ABOUT IT.

I'VE BEEN DOING IT EVER SINCE I WAS A CHILD. THERE'S NOT MUCH ELSE I CAN DO WITH THESE BIG DUMB HANDS.

HEY, BIG HANDS!

KEEP DRUMMING, YOU DIM-WITTED MUTANT!

YIKES! THAT WASN'T VERY NICE. DOES HE ALWAYS CALL YOU NAMES?

YEAH. I GUESS IT'S JUST PART OF THE JOB.

BUT NOW I MUST DRUM UNTIL THE NOISE MAKES YOU BANG YOUR HEAD AGAINST THE WALL!

SORRY. IT'S NOT PERSONAL.

BOOM-BOOM!
BOOM-BOOM!

IF YOU WEREN'T LOCKED UP IN THIS DARK ROOM AND COULD DRUM OUTSIDE, I BET LOTS OF PEOPLE WOULD LOVE YOUR DRUMMING!

AND THERE'S LOTS OF STUFF THOSE BIG HANDS COULD BE USED FOR. YOU COULD HOLD BIG THINGS AND OPEN TIGHT JARS, AND I BET YOU'D BE GREAT AT CLAPPING AND GIVING AWESOME HIGH FIVES.

WHAT ARE HIGH FIVES?

PUT YOUR HAND UP LIKE THIS . . .

OK.

WHEN SOMETHING COOL HAPPENS, WE GIVE EACH OTHER A "HIGH FIVE"!

SMACK!
THAT'S FUN!

WHAT ARE
THEY DOING?

DRUM, YOU
KNUCKLEHEAD, DRUM!
BOOM-BOOM!

BOOM-BOOM!

BOOM-BA-BOOM!
BOOM-BA-BOOM!

CHAPTER 13

THAT LITTLE MUCK-HEADED KID HAS BEEN DANCING IN THE BOOM ROOM ALL NIGHT . . . NO ONE HAS EVER LASTED THAT LONG.

THAT'S ENOUGH BOOMING.

YOU CAN STOP NOW.

FRED, YOU CAN STOP DANCING.
BUT I STILL HEAR THE BEAT IN MY HEAD.

YOU PUT THE FUNK IN ME.

COME WITH US, KID!

SMACK!
GOODBYE!

FREDDY BOOM-BOOM! SOLE SURVIVOR OF THE BOOM ROOM! YOU'RE A PRETTY TOUGH KID. I LIKE THAT. Y'KNOW, I WAS THINKING ABOUT WHAT YOU SAID ABOUT ME AND LORD BONKERS. MAYBE YOU'RE RIGHT, KIDDO! MAYBE WE SHOULD JUST . . . STOP!

REALLY? THAT'S AMAZING! YOU WON'T EVER REGRET DOING SOMETHING GOOD.

WOW! THIS IS REALLY THOUGHTFUL OF YOU. I'M SURE THIS WILL HELP YOU TWO BECOME FRIENDS.

GOODBYE, EVERYONE!

URGH . . . URGH . . .

OOOF!

UUUNGH!

IT'S STUCK.

WHAT DO I
DO NOW?

VROOOOM!
?

HELLO?
HELLO!

VROOOOOOOM!

I'M OVER
HERE!

JUNKBOY!
FRED!

NEED A
LIFT?

THAT WOULD
BE GREAT.

I WAS HOPING
I'D RUN INTO
YOU AGAIN!

AFTER OUR TALK, I MADE MORE HELMETS, AND PEOPLE STARTED TO BUY THEM. THEN I BOUGHT THIS RIG, AND NOW I TRAVEL AROUND SELLING MY HELMETS.

GOOD FOR YOU.

AND SINCE WE MET, I HAVEN'T STOLEN ANYTHING.

I KNEW YOU COULD DO IT.

LET'S GO.

WE'D BETTER PUT ON OUR SEAT BELTS.
WHAT'S A SEAT BELT?

VROOOM!

HEY, WHAT'S THAT?

LET'S FIND OUT.

WORMY! YOU ESCAPED!
I ALWAYS DO.

C'MON, GET IN.

YEAH . . . MAYBE A RIDE WOULD BE NICE.

GUESS WHAT? I'M GOING BACK TO SEE LORD BONKERS!

OH, FRED . . .

VROOOM!

CHAPTER 14

YOU AGAIN? GUARDS! GET THE BOOT READY!
WAIT! I'VE BROUGHT SOMETHING FOR YOU!

I HOPE IT'S NOT ANOTHER DUMB FACE ROCK!

IS THIS A TRICK?
NO.

I ASKED HIM TO STOP FIGHTING WITH YOU, AND HE SAID THAT SOUNDED GOOD, AND HE SENT THIS TO YOU.
TAP! TAP! TAP!

HE'S NOT SUCH A BAD GUY.

SQUEAK!

YOU SAID THIS WASN'T A TRICK.

IT'S NOT.

CREAK!

SQUEAK!

CREAK!

WHAT DOES IT SAY?

"YOU SMELL
LIKE POOP!"
OH! THAT
CAN'T
BE RIGHT.

"YOU SMELL
LIKE POOP!"

YOU HAVE INSULTED ME
FOR THE LAST TIME, FRED!
WHAM!

I'M SO SORRY! PAPA
MAYHEM REALLY
SEEMED LIKE HE
WANTED TO BE PALS!

MAYHEM IS EVIL! HE
CANNOT BE TRUSTED!

YOU'RE GOING TO PAY FOR THIS, FRED! GUARDS! TAKE HIM TO THE ARENA!

IT'S CRUSHING TIME!
CRUSHING TIME!

CRUSHING TIME?
YEAH, FRED! CRUSHING TIME!

CRUSHING TIME!
BWA!
BWAA!

CRUSHING TIME!
AM I THE ONE GETTING CRUSHED?

THAT'S RIGHT, KID! YOU'RE GONNA GET SOOOO CRUSHED!
CLANK!

CRUSHING TIME!

CRUSHING TIME!
CRUSHING TIME!
GATHER 'ROUND AND CHECK IT OUT! THIS LITTLE GUY IS GONNA SCREAM AND SHOUT! HE'S GONNA GET SQUASHED, HE'S GONNA GO SPLAT . . .

. . . THIS LITTLE PUNK NAMED FRED . . .
. . . IS GONNA BE FLAT!

HOORAY!
OPEN THE GATE!
LET THE CRUSHING BEGIN!

!
RRRRRRRRR
1

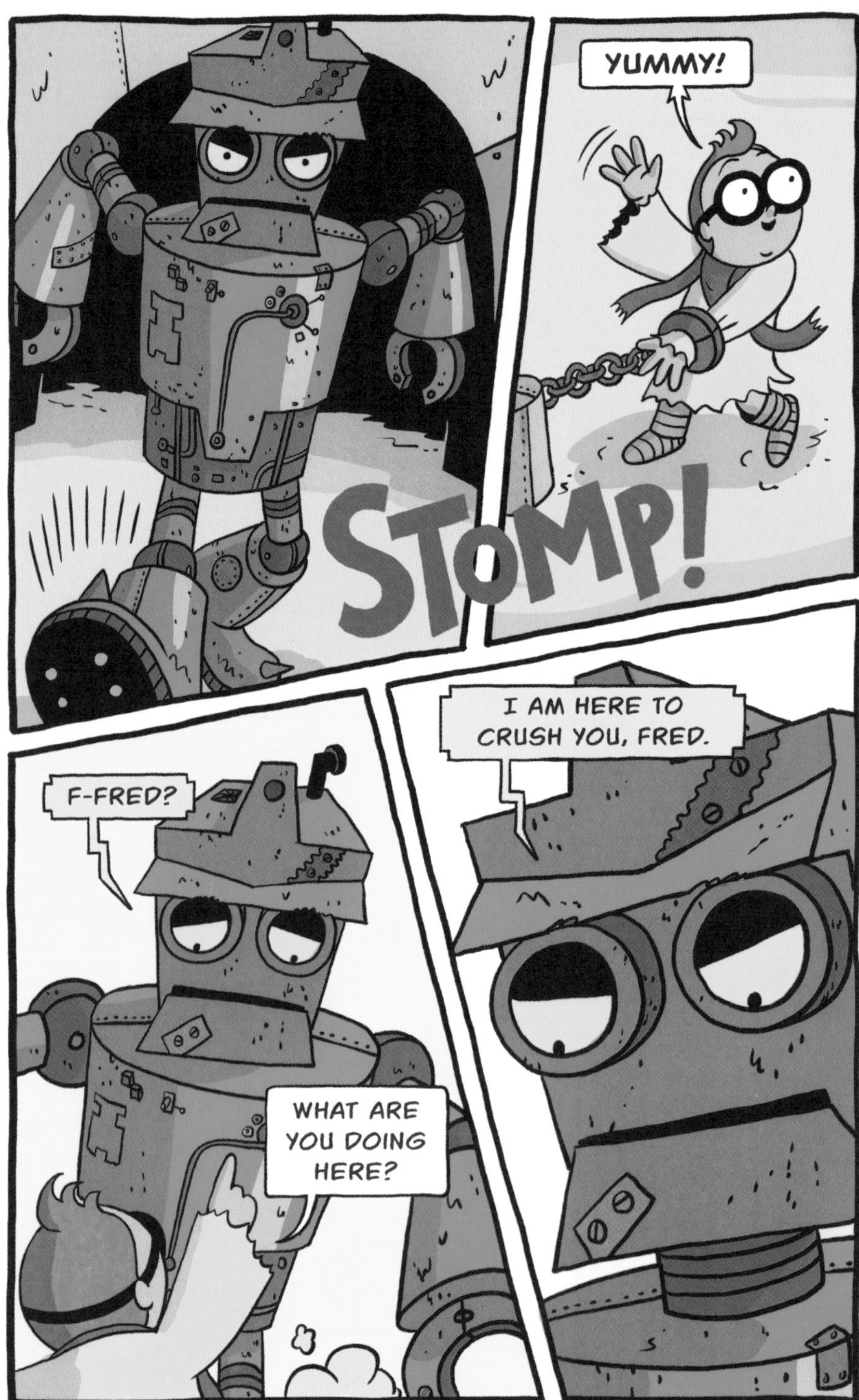
YUMMY!
STOMP!
F-FRED?
I AM HERE TO CRUSH YOU, FRED.
WHAT ARE YOU DOING HERE?

BUT . . . BUT WE'RE FRIENDS.
YES. WE ARE.
THEN . . . MAYBE YOU WON'T CRUSH ME?
I AM A CRUSHER. I AM JUST DOING MY JOB, FRED. IT IS NOT PERSONAL.
CRUSH HIM, YOU METAL GOON!
BUT I HELPED YOU.

CRUSH HIM!
CLICK!

NO! I WILL NOT CRUSH FRED! HE IS FULL OF KINDNESS AND GOODNESS! HE HELPS THOSE WHO ARE IN NEED AND ASKS NOTHING IN RETURN!

BOO!
FINE. BE THAT WAY. OPEN GATE NUMBER TWO!
UH-OH!

CLANK! CLANK!
HOORAY!
BLUE ROBOT!
DESTROY
RED ROBOT!
SPLAP!
NO!

CRASH!
YUMMY! ARE YOU OK?
BLUE ROBOT! CRUSH THE KID!
CLANK!
CLANK!
CLANK!

WHAM!
CLINK!
BLAM!
DONK!
CLANK!
CLONK!

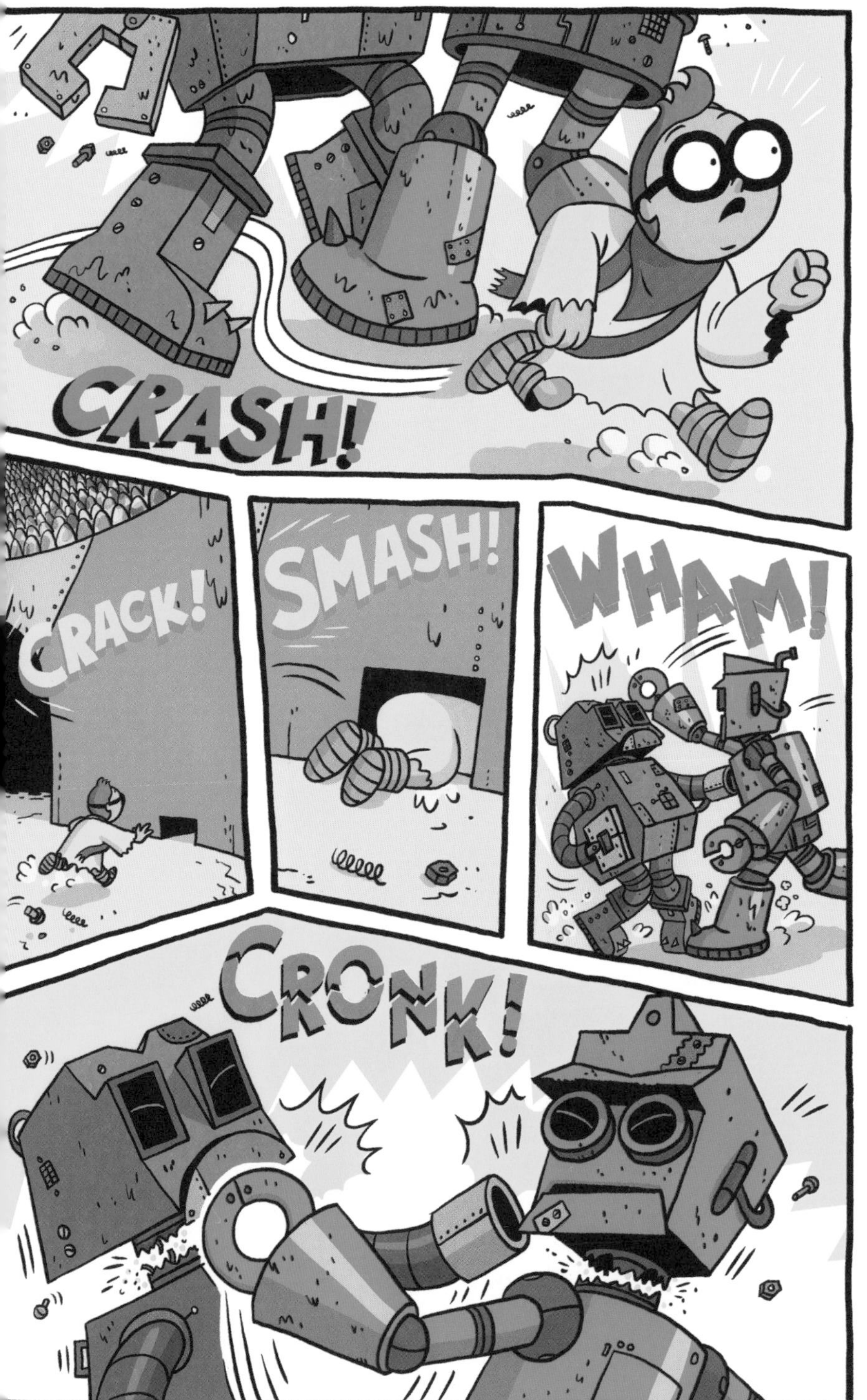
CRASH!
CRACK!
SMASH!
WHAM!
CRONK!

BZZZT!
OH YEAH!
HOORAY!
WHAM!
WHERE'S FRED? WHERE'D HE GO?
FIND FRED! FIND HIM NOW!

CHAPTER 15

OH, HELLO.
SHHHH! YOU BE QUIET, OR THEY'LL FIND US!

OK.

ARE YOU IN TROUBLE?
YES, I AM.

YOU CAN STAY HERE WITH US IF YOU WANT. NO ONE WILL FIND YOU DOWN HERE.
THANK YOU.

DO YOU MIND IF I ASK A QUESTION?

AS LONG AS IT'S NOT A STUPID QUESTION.

I'LL DO MY BEST. WHAT HAPPENED TO THE WORLD?

WHAT DO YOU MEAN, "WHAT HAPPENED?"

IT'S DIFFERENT NOW. IT WASN'T ALWAYS LIKE THIS.

THERE WAS
A GREAT WAR.

THEN THERE
WAS NO
WATER.

THEN A
COMET HIT
THE WORLD.

THEN THE
ALIENS CAME.

THEN
ANOTHER
WAR.

THEN THE
ROBOTS
TOOK OVER.

ANOTHER
COMET.

ANOTHER
WAR.

THAT'S A
LOT OF
BAD STUFF.

NO WONDER THINGS ARE THE WAY THEY ARE.

OH! THE CATS! DON'T FORGET THE CATS!

MILLIONS AND MILLIONS OF CATS!

THEY WERE EVERYWHERE!

SHREDDING EVERYTHING!

OH! THE CONSTANT MEOWING!

AND THEY PEED ON EVERYTHING!

THE WORLD STANK OF CAT PEE!

THAT SMELL! THAT TERRIBLE SMELL!

BLAM!
RUN!
HUH?
ZIP!
UH-OH!

I GOT
YOU, FRED!

BUT TODAY'S
YOUR LUCKY
DAY!

I'VE BEEN THINKING ABOUT WHAT
YOU SAID, AND I'VE SENT
A MESSENGER TO MAKE A PEACE
OFFERING TO PAPA MAYHEM!

THAT'S AMAZING!
WHAT MADE YOU
CHANGE YOUR
MIND?

YOU! YOUR KINDNESS CAUSED
A CRUSH-BOT NOT TO CRUSH!
THAT'S SOME HEAVY-DUTY
GOODNESS, FRED!

WOW! THANKS!
AND ONE MORE THING, MY ODD LITTLE FRIEND. YOU'RE GOING TO OVERSEE THE SIGNING OF THE PEACE TREATY!

ME? REALLY?

YUP, FREDDY BOY! IT'S GOING TO BE AMAZING!

IT WILL BE A PRIVILEGE! AND HERE'S SOMETHING JUST FOR YOU!

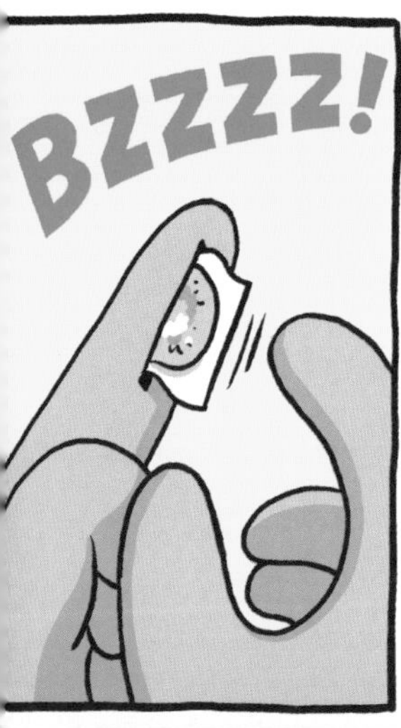

YOU'RE THE COOLEST!

CHAPTER 16

THEY'RE REALLY MEAN MEN, FRED. THEY'RE PROUD TO CALL THEMSELVES WARLORDS.

BUT I COULDN'T FIND ANY FLOUR.

OR SUGAR.

OR BUTTER.

OR CHOCOLATE CHIPS.

HELLO!
FREDDY!

I'M SO HAPPY YOU BOTH CAME! BUT I KNEW YOU WOULD, EVEN IF MY FRIEND WORMY SAID YOU WOULDN'T.

I'M LEAVING!
PFT!

EXCUSE ME!
HUH?
BUMP!

SO, SHOULD WE JUST SIGN THIS, OR IS THERE ANYTHING YOU WANT TO SAY?
PEACE

FRED, I ADMIRE YOUR DETERMINATION AND SPUNK! YOU TRULY ARE A FORCE OF NATURE.

YES, MANY KOOKY PEOPLE HAVE TRIED, BUT NO ONE HAS EVER GOTTEN US TO MEET FACE-TO-FACE.

AND NO ONE HAS EVER GOTTEN US TO AGREE TO A TREATY! TO PROVE MY DEDICATION TO LIVING IN PEACE AND HARMONY, I HAVE SOMETHING FOR PAPA MAYHEM.
HAPPY PEACE DAY

A GIFT? THAT IS SO NICE!

BEHOLD! THE DESTRUCTO-DOME!

RUMBLE
RUMBL

THAT'S AN
ODD PRESENT.

HA! IT IS NO MATCH
FOR MY MURDER-CUBE!

VRRR

THEY DON'T LOOK LIKE
GIFTS . . . THEY LOOK LIKE
WEAPONS! AND SOLDIERS!
WHAT'S GOING ON?

AMAZING!
GLORIOUS!

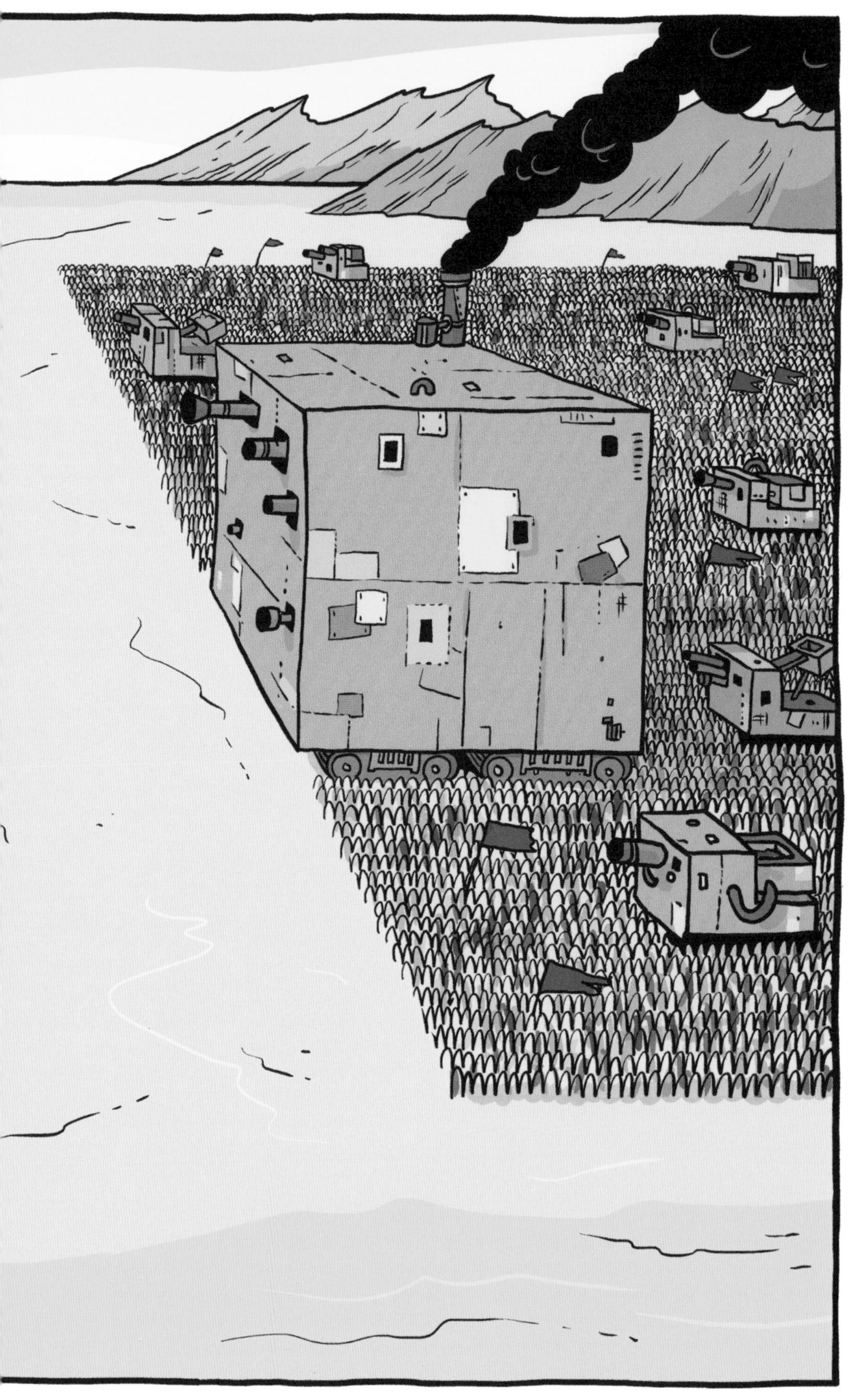

FRED, YOU MUST BE A BLOCKHEAD TO THINK THAT AFTER ALL THE YEARS WE'VE BEEN ENEMIES, YOU'RE GOING TO COME ALONG AND GET US TO STOP FIGHTING . . . JUST BY ASKING?

YOU THINK WE'RE GONNA BE **PALS**?

HA!

YOU SAID YOU WOULD STOP! YOU SAID YOU WANTED TO SIGN THE PEACE TREATY!

HA! HA! HA!

WE LIED!

YOU GULLIBLE LITTLE FOOL! WE JUST AGREED TO WHAT YOU WANTED SO WE COULD ORGANIZE OUR ARMIES!
AND PREPARE FOR WAR!
AND MAKE YOU WATCH!
OPEN FIRE!
PLOK!
PLOK!
PLOK!

OH NO!
LET THEM HAVE IT!
FOOZ!
FOOZ!
SPLOP!
MAKE THEM STOP!
FIRE THE SLIMERS!

SKWEEP!
SPLOP!
SPLORP!
GREASE GUNS! FIRE!
I'LL DO ANYTHING! JUST PLEASE STOP FIGHTING!
FOOZ! FOOZ!
SPLOK!

IT DOESN'T HAVE TO BE LIKE THIS!
BWAM! BWAM! BWAM!
YOU DON'T NEED TO FIGHT!
SPLOO!
PLOOM!
SPLOP!

WHAM!
PLOOM!

ZOOF!
FLOOM!
STOP! EVERYBODY, PLEASE STOP!
SPLORP!

PUT DOWN YOUR WEAPONS!
YOU CAN STOP IF YOU WANT!
AWW! HE'S TRYING TO STOP THEM! SUCH A SWEET BOY!
BOO-HOO! HE DOESN'T LIKE ALL THE MEAN PEOPLE FIGHTING!
MUCK SHOOTERS! FIRE!
SLUDGE CANNONS! FIRE!
PLOK!
SPLAM!

BLAM!
PLEASE! ALL OF YOU! JUST STOP!
TRASH CATAPULTS, GO!
FOOSH!
JUNK TOSSERS, GO!
FWAM!

BLAM!
SPLAP!
SKWEE!
SPLORP!
ZOOF! ZOOF!
BAM!
CLONK!

IT'S BEAUTIFUL, ISNT IT?

I'VE NEVER SEEN A LOVELIER SIGHT!
YOU KNOW, I'M GOING TO WIN!

NO, YOU'RE NOT! THE SPOON OF TRUTH TOLD ME I WOULD WIN!
THE *WHAT?*

THE SPOON OF TRUTH! IT GIVES ME GUIDANCE! IT TOLD ME I WOULD KICK YOUR GREASY BUTT!

SOUNDS LIKE A STUPID SPOON!

I DARE YOU TO TELL THAT TO THE SPOON!

IT'S GONE! THE SPOON OF TRUTH IS GONE!

YOU STOLE MY SPOON!

I DID NOT! I CAN WIN WITHOUT STEALING YOUR LYING SPOON!

GIVE IT BACK!

BLAM!
DONK!
SPLOO!
BAM!
POW!
BONK!

EVERYBODY! LISTEN UP! YOU DON'T HAVE TO FIGHT!
PLOO!
BWAP!
SPLORP!
FRED?
I DIDN'T TAKE YOUR SPOON!
YES, YOU DID!
HEH!

SPLOP!
THIS IS TERRIBLE? WHAT HAVE I DONE?
SPLAP!
HI, GREASY MO!
AWW! NO ONE HAS EVER REMEMBERED MY NAME BEFORE!
SPWAM!

FOR THE LAST TIME, MAYHEM . . .
. . . I DIDN'T TAKE YOUR STUPID TALKING . . .
. . . SPOON!
BAM!
FWOO!

IGGY?
HOW DO YOU KNOW MY NAME?
BECAUSE I'M . . . ZIGGY.
I THOUGHT YOU DIED YEARS AGO!
I THOUGHT YOU WERE DEAD TOO!

BROTHER!

I THOUGHT I'D NEVER SEE YOU AGAIN! WAH!

WAH! ME TOO! WAH!

SPLOP!
PLEASE! CAN'T EVERYONE JUST BE NICE?
FRED!
CHUK!
AFTER I LOST YOU, I BECAME MEAN! I HATED EVERYTHING AND EVERYBODY!
ME TOO! I WANTED EVERYONE ELSE TO FEEL AS ROTTEN AS I FELT!

IF IT WEREN'T FOR FRED, WE WOULD HAVE NEVER FOUND EACH OTHER.
SWEET, KOOKY FRED. HEY, WHERE IS HE?

PLEASE STOP FIGHTIIIING!
FRED?

OH NO!
YIKES!

CEASE FIRE!
STAND DOWN!

CHAPTER 17

SO, UM, HEH. . . THIS IS A FUNNY STORY. IT TURNS OUT THAT LORD BONKERS AND I ARE, UM, LONG-LOST BROTHERS!
PRETTY WILD, HUH?

AND SINCE WE'RE BROTHERS, UH . . . WE'RE NOT GOING TO BE FIGHTING ANYMORE. OK?
YEAH, SO . . . YOU'RE ALL FRIENDS NOW!

GO ON! BE FRIENDLY!

SORRY I SLIMED YOU.
IT'S OK. SORRY I GREASED YOU.

SORRY I BONKED YOU.
EH, IT HAPPENS.

AND FROM NOW ON, THERE WILL BE PEACE THROUGHOUT THE VALLEY! AND, UH . . .

...YOU'RE ALL FREE!
HOORAY!
HOORAY!
AND IT'S ALL BECAUSE OF OUR PAL FRED! YOU CAN COME OUT NOW, FRED. IT'S SAFE!

WE'VE GOT TO FIND HIM!

FRED!

HAS ANYONE SEEN FRED? HE'S A LITTLE GUY WITH BIG GOGGLES?
HE WEARS A YELLOW SHIRT AND HAS BLUE HAIR?

AND HE'S A REALLY GREAT DANCER?

I SAW HIM! HE WENT THAT WAY!

HE WENT TOWARD THE MUCK VATS!

HIS GOGGLES!

HIS SCARF!

OH NO! HE'S IN THE VAT!

HURRY!

FRED!
ARE YOU IN THERE?

C'MON! FIND HIM!
GIMME A SECOND!

I GOT HIM!

BUT HE'S STUCK!

PULL!
UUGH!
OOGH!
UNH!
SPLORP!

FRED? CAN YOU HEAR ME?
FRED?

RUB! RUB! RUB!

WAKE UP, FRED!

WHA . . . WHAT HAPPENED?

YOU WERE STUCK!

STUCK?

IN THE MUCK!

I WAS STUCK? IN THE MUCK?

YUCK.

TEE-HEE-HEE!

I MADE A SILLY RHYME.

THE LITTLE GOOFBALL IS FINE!

HEY, WHAT ARE YOU DOING HERE?
I PULLED YOU OUT OF THE MUCK.

YOU WERE RIGHT! THESE BIG DUMB HANDS CAN DO GOOD THINGS!

ALL RIGHT! HIGH FIVE!
SMACK!

WHAT WAS THAT?

THAT'S A HIGH FIVE. FRIENDS DO IT WHEN SOMETHING COOL HAPPENS!

SHOULD WE?

SMACK!

HEY! YOU TWO LOOK LIKE EACH OTHER.

YEAH, WE DO!
WE'RE LONG-LOST BROTHERS.

TWINS, ACTUALLY.
AWW, THAT'S NICE!

FRED!

PUG!
PLUG!

THIS IS ALL SO NICE! I GUESS THINGS HAVE WORKED OUT AFTER ALL.

SMACK!

SMACK!

SMACK!
SMACK!
SMACK!
SMACK!
SMACK!

CHAPTER 18

I'VE BEEN LOOKING ALL OVER FOR YOU.
WELL, YOU FOUND ME.

SO, THERE'S GOING TO BE PEACE NOW.

YUP! AND NONE OF THIS WOULD HAVE HAPPENED IF I HADN'T SNATCHED *THIS!*

YOU STOLE IT?

I SURE DID! AFTER ALL OF YOUR HARD WORK, IT WAS THIS DOPEY LITTLE THING THAT BROUGHT THEM TOGETHER. YOU CAN THANK ME FOR THE PEACE **YOU'VE** CREATED.

YOU WEREN'T HELPING ME, YOU WERE USING ME.

WELL, I DID SAY YOU OWED ME ONE.

THE MINUTE I MET YOU, FRED, I KNEW YOU WERE SPECIAL.

I KNEW THAT WHEREVER YOU WENT, THERE WOULD BE CHAOS. AND CHAOS IS A THIEF'S BEST FRIEND. WHEN EVERYONE WAS WATCHING YOU TALKING ABOUT YOUR INSANE PEACE PLAN, NO ONE WAS WATCHING ME!

OH . . .

THEN WE'RE NOT FRIENDS?

NO. WE'RE NOT FRIENDS.

WE'RE PARTNERS!

YOU KNOW, FRED, YOUR PROGRAMMING FORGOT ONE IMPORTANT THING.

SOME PEOPLE JUST DON'T WANT TO BE PALS.

WAIT . . .

BZZZZ!

THIS IS FOR YOU. YOU HELPED IN YOUR OWN SPECIAL WAY.

I BEE-LIEVE IN YOU!

THANK YOU, WORMY.

WHATEVER, FREDDY BOY!

CHAPTER 19

YOU'RE WELCOME TO STAY HERE WITH US.
THANK YOU, BUT I THINK I SHOULD MOVE ON.

THERE ARE A LOT OF PEOPLE OUT THERE WHO NEED A PAL, SO I'M JUST GOING TO WANDER AROUND . . . AND SEE WHO I CAN HELP.

THAT'S MIGHTY NOBLE OF YOU, FRED.

WILL YOU TWO PROMISE TO HELP ALL THE PEOPLE YOU HAVE HURT?

YES. THERE'S A LOT OF THINGS WE HAVE TO FIX.
AND A LOT OF STUFF WE NEED TO MAKE RIGHT.

GOOD FOR YOU!

WELL, IT WAS A PLEASURE TO MEET EACH AND EVERY ONE OF YOU.

GOODBYE, FRED!

GOODBYE!

BE SAFE, FRED!

STAY OUT OF THE RADIATION ZONE! IT'S FULL OF RADIATION!

STAY OUT OF THE POISON ZONE! IT'S FULL OF POISON!

STAY OUT OF THE TURD ZONE!
IT'S FULL OF TURDS!

LA LA LA . . .

LEE LA LOO . . .
LEE LEE LEE . . .
HUH?
DO YOU LIKE IT?
JUNKBOY! I LOVE IT! IT'S AMAZING! DID YOU MAKE IT?

YUP! I USED ALL THE JUNK LEFT OUT ON THE BATTLEFIELD.

I KNEW YOU HAD A HEAD FULL OF GREAT IDEAS.

ACTUALLY, IT WASN'T MY IDEA. I'M REALLY NOT SUPPOSED TO TELL YOU, BUT . . .

. . . IT WAS WORMY'S IDEA.

WORMY?

BE
KIND
SHE'S FULL
OF SURPRISES,
ISN'T SHE?
YES . . . SHE
REALLY IS.

SMACK!

GOODBYE!

BE KIND
LEE LEE LEE . . .

LA LA LA . . . .

Mike Rex 2021

Fred's Guide to Making Friends

If you want to learn how to make friends like Fred, here are a few simple steps you can try!

STEP #1

Notice what someone is interested in.

STEP #2

Ask a question about that interest.

STEP #3

Compliment the person on their interest.

STEP #4

Introduce yourself and ask the other person their name.

STEP #5

Tell a joke.
(If you can make the joke related to their interest, that's even better.)

STEP #6

Smile.

(This is the easiest step.)

Summer 2020
Photo credit: M. Rex

MICHAEL REX has been writing and illustrating since 1995 and has created over forty-five books for children, including the #1 bestseller and Halloween favorite *Goodnight Goon*. His Fangbone! graphic novels have been adapted into an animated TV show, and his recent picture book *Facts vs. Opinions vs. Robots* is being developed for TV as well. He's written for all ages, from simple picture books such as *Eat Pete* to the illustrated chapter book series Icky Ricky. He travels the country talking about his work with students of all ages, has a master's degree in arts education, and also taught high school art for three years in the Bronx.

He has been obsessed with postapocalyptic stories since he was young, and has wanted to tell a story like *Your Pal Fred* as long as he can remember. He lives in New Jersey with his wife, two teenage boys, and a dog named Roxy.

Visit him on Twitter @mikerexbooks, Instagram @fangbone_rex, or at mikerexbooks.blogspot.com.